Honor
the Happy Days
Fairy

Special thanks to
Narinder Dhami

ORCHARD BOOKS
338 Euston Road, London NW1 3BH
Orchard Books Australia
Level 17/207 Kent Street, Sydney, NSW 2000
A Paperback Original

First published in 2011 by Orchard Books

© 2011 Rainbow Magic Limited.
A HIT Entertainment company. Rainbow Magic
is a trademark of Rainbow Magic Limited.
Reg. U.S. Pat. & Tm. Off. And other countries.
www.rainbowmagiconline.com

HiT entertainment

Illustrations © Orchard Books 2011

A CIP catalogue record for this book is available
from the British Library.

ISBN 978 1 40831 293 3

1 3 5 7 9 10 8 6 4 2

Printed in Great Britain

The paper and board used in this paperback are natural recyclable
products made from wood grown in sustainable forests. The
manufacturing processes conform to the environmental regulations
of the country of origin.

Orchard Books is a division of Hachette Children's Books,
an Hachette UK company

www.hachette.co.uk

Honor
the Happy Days
Fairy

by Daisy Meadows

ORCHARD BOOKS

www.rainbowmagic.co.uk

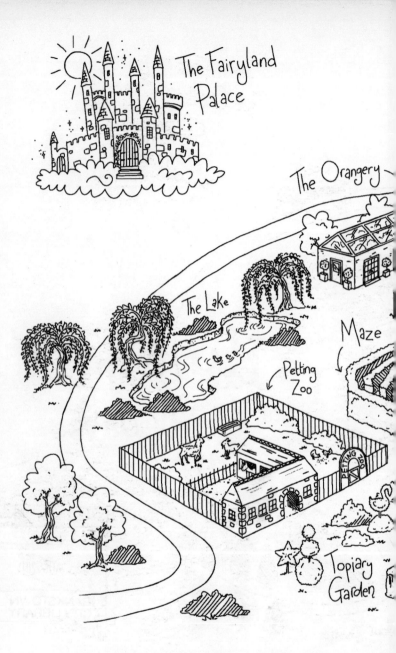

The Fairyland Palace

The Orangery

The Lake

Maze

Petting Zoo

PETTING ZOO

Topiary Garden

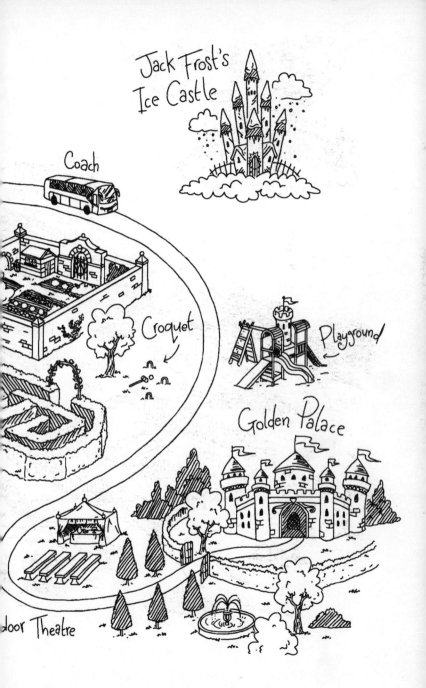

The fairies are planning a magical ball,
With guests of honour and fun for them all.
They're expecting a night full of laughter and cheer
But they'll get a shock when my goblins appear!

Adventures and treats will be things of the past,
And I'll beat those troublesome fairies at last.
My iciest magic will blast through the room
And the world will be plunged into grimness
and gloom!

Contents

Princess Rachel and Princess Kirsty!

"We're here, Kirsty!" Rachel bounced up and down in her seat with excitement as she pointed out of the coach window. "Look, that sign says *Golden Palace*."

Kirsty beamed at her friend. "I can't believe we get to spend a whole week in a *real* palace," she sighed happily. "I'm beginning to feel like a princess already!"

There were cheers
and whoops as the
other children on the
coach also spotted
the sign. Golden Palace,
a large and beautiful stately home, was
in the countryside just outside the village
of Wetherbury, which was where Kirsty
lived. The house was open to the public,
but Kirsty had never visited it before.
However, during the spring holidays the
house was holding a special Kids' Week,
and Kirsty had invited Rachel to come to
Golden Palace with her.

"I can't wait to see our bedroom,"
Rachel said eagerly as the coach drove
through the tall wrought-iron gates.
"Imagine staying in a room that was
once used by princes and princesses!"

"And I wonder what activities we're going to be doing this week," Kirsty added. "I hope we get to do lots of princess-type things!"

The coach trundled over a drawbridge and then began to wind its way slowly through the enormous grounds. Like all the other children on the coach, Rachel and Kirsty stared excitedly out of the window, straining to catch their first glimpse of Golden Palace.

GOLDEN PALACE

But there were lots of amazing things on the way to the house that caught their attention, too.

"Look, a petting zoo!" Kirsty exclaimed as they drove past a field of tiny Shetland ponies and little white goats. The girls could also see another field with horses and donkeys grazing, and pens of baby piglets, rabbits and guinea pigs. "Aren't the Shetland ponies cute?"

"There's a lake just over there," Rachel pointed out. The lake was surrounded by beautiful willow trees, and ducks and swans were gliding across the water. "And look at that *enormous* white greenhouse, Kirsty.

I can see lots of orange and lemon trees growing inside it."

"I think it's called an orangery," Kirsty replied. "I've seen one before, when my family visited another stately home."

The coach passed a croquet field with hoops stuck into the grass, and then a very big, complicated maze made of close-growing green hedges.

"That maze has lots of twists and turns," Rachel whispered to Kirsty. "We might get lost in it and need some fairy magic to find our way out!"

The two girls exchanged a smile. Their friendship with the fairies was a very special secret.

The coach moved on through ornamental gardens that were so beautiful, the girls caught their breath in awe. There were huge flowerbeds filled with dazzling colour, topiary figures cut out of hedges, marble statues, fishponds with fountains, and peacocks wandering here and there. Everyone on the coach, including Rachel and Kirsty, applauded as one of the peacocks spread open his magnificent blue and green tail.

"Here's Golden Palace, just ahead of us," the coach driver called.

Rachel and Kirsty saw an enormous building made of white stone that gleamed in the sunshine. The palace had

four high towers, one at each corner of
the building, and a fifth tower, the highest
one, right in the centre. The towers were
surrounded by golden turrets, and each
one had a flag flying on top of it.

"This is brilliant, Rachel!" Kirsty
breathed, her eyes wide with delight.
"I can't wait to explore the palace
tomorrow."

"It looks like something from a fairytale, doesn't it?" the girl sitting in front of them remarked. Rachel and Kirsty grinned at each other.

"Maybe we'll see some of our fairy friends during our stay here!" Rachel whispered.

The coach drew to a halt outside the palace entrance with its marble pillars, and everyone began collecting up their bags. As Rachel and Kirsty climbed off the coach with the others, a woman hurried out of the palace, followed by a young man. They both wore smart navy-blue trouser suits with gold buttons.

"Hi, everyone!" called the woman with a welcoming smile. "I'm Caroline, and this is Louis. We're your palace stewards, and we'll be looking after you during your stay."

"We know you're going to *love* your week here at Golden Palace," Louis added. "So let's get the fun started straightaway! The coach driver will bring in your bags while Caroline and I show you around."

Kirsty and Rachel moved forward through the doors, eager like everyone else to get their first glimpse of Golden Palace. To their delight, the girls found themselves in a large and very beautiful reception hall. The hall had tall, arched windows, a marble floor and a high ceiling decorated with painted plaster flowers and birds.

The walls were panelled in rich, dark
wood. A giant chandelier hung from the
middle of the ceiling, its crystal drops
twinkling like diamonds in the
sunlight that streamed through
the windows. At the opposite
end of the hall was a
curving staircase made
of pale pink and white
marble that swept regally
up to the top floor.

"This is *just* what a
palace should be like!"
Rachel murmured to
Kirsty who nodded.

"You'll have plenty of time
to yourselves to explore the
palace while you're here," Louis said.
He waved a hand at the marble stairs.

"Now this is called the *grand* staircase!" he explained. "This is the staircase that the princes and princesses would have used. There's another set of stairs for the servants!"

As they all gazed up at the impressive staircase, Rachel and Kirsty were interested to see that the walls along the stairs were hung with old portraits in gilt frames.

"These pictures are of people who used to live here in the palace," Caroline told them.

"Who's that?" asked Kirsty as she spotted a picture of a girl in a Victorian crinoline who looked about the same age as she and Rachel.

"That's Princess Charlotte," Caroline replied. "She lived here about one hundred and thirty years ago."

"Caroline and I should warn you that Golden Palace is full of mysterious secrets," Louis said with a twinkle in his eye. "There are hidden passages and sliding bookcases and secret drawers in the furniture and all sorts of other amazing things to find!" He pushed one corner of the wooden panel closest

to him. Everyone gasped in astonishment as a whole long length of panelling moved aside, revealing a dark passageway behind it.

"This is going to be the most brilliant fun!" Rachel said to Kirsty. "*And* we get to be princesses for a week!"

"You're allowed to go pretty much wherever you like in the palace," Louis explained, "Except for the highest tower. That's crumbling away a little, so it's not safe."

"Right, time for supper," Caroline announced, leading the way down the corridor. "Then we'll show you to your rooms and you can settle down for the night."

After a supper of cheese on toast and mugs of creamy hot chocolate in the beautiful banqueting room, Caroline took Rachel and Kirsty to their bedchamber.

It was richly decorated in shades of blue and gold, and it had twin four-poster beds with matching bedspreads printed with a pattern of peacock feathers. A silver and glass chandelier hung from the ceiling, shimmering in the light.

"See you tomorrow, girls," Caroline called as she closed the door behind her.

"Isn't this gorgeous?" Rachel said, gazing at the four-poster beds. "It's just like being real princesses! But I suppose we'd better unpack before we go to sleep, Kirsty."

"Do princesses do their own unpacking?" Kirsty asked with a grin. She glanced up to admire the chandelier and suddenly the smile disappeared from her face. She frowned, looking puzzled. "Rachel, I'm sure that chandelier has got much brighter since we came in!"

Rachel also gazed upwards. "You're right, Kirsty," she exclaimed, shading her eyes. "It's so bright now, I can hardly look at it!"

At that moment a tiny sparkling figure spun out of the middle of the shimmering chandelier and danced through the air towards them.

"It's a fairy, Rachel!" Kirsty gasped. "It's our old friend, Polly the Party Fun Fairy!"

Enter the Princess Fairies

"Yes, it's me, girls!" Polly zoomed down towards them, her long red curls flying, and beamed at Rachel and Kirsty. "I've been sent by King Oberon and Queen Titania to bring you a *very* special invitation. Would you like to come to a Fairyland ball?"

The girls looked thrilled.

"Of course we would!" Rachel cried.

"That's the answer I was hoping for,"
Polly laughed. "Get ready, then – off we
go to Fairyland. One, two, three!"

Polly flicked her wand in the air,
sending showers of glittering fairy dust
swirling around the girls.
Instantly Rachel and
Kirsty felt themselves
spinning through the
air as Polly's magic
whizzed them away
to Fairyland.

Just a few seconds
later, Rachel, Kirsty
and Polly arrived outside the Fairyland
Palace with its golden towers. The girls
were delighted to see that all their fairy
friends were waiting there, along with the
king and queen.

"Welcome, Rachel and Kirsty!" King Oberon announced with a smile.

"We're so glad you could join us for this very special ball, girls," Queen Titania added, and the other fairies clapped and cheered. "Thank you for coming."

"Thank you for inviting us!" said Kirsty.

"But why is it a very *special* ball, Your Majesty?" Rachel wanted to know.

"Because, besides yourselves, we're waiting for some *very* honoured guests," the queen explained. "The seven Princess Fairies should be here any moment now!"

"The Princess Fairies are our cousins," King Oberon explained. "They live far away in a distant land."

Suddenly the clip-clop of horses' hooves could be heard in the distance.

"That must be the Princess Fairies' carriage!" the queen exclaimed. "Where's Bertram?"

Bertram the frog footman hopped forward. "Here, Your Majesty."

"All the footmen must be ready to receive the Princesses," the queen told him. Rachel and Kirsty glanced round and saw a group of footmen hanging around in the background, their caps pulled down low over their faces.

A glass carriage drawn by two snow-white horses was now approaching the palace. As Rachel and Kirsty watched, the coach drew to a halt and Bertram sprang forward to open the door. He helped the Princess Fairies out one by one as the watching crowd, including the girls, applauded loudly.

"Aren't their ballgowns gorgeous?" Kirsty whispered to Rachel.

"And look at their tiaras!" Rachel whispered back. "They're so sparkly, and each one has a different-shaped jewel in the centre."

"Welcome, Princess Fairies!" Queen Titania announced. "It's wonderful to see you all again."

"Please follow us to the royal ballroom," King Oberon announced, "And let the ball begin!"

The king and queen led the way to the ballroom, with Polly the Party Fun Fairy, Rachel and Kirsty following closely behind them.

Bertram escorted the Princess Fairies to the ballroom.

Meanwhile, the other footmen were left to look after the horses and the glass coach.

"Oh, this is magical!" Rachel gasped as Polly showed them into the ballroom. The pink and gold room was lit with candles and festooned with garlands of sweetly scented white flowers. A fairy orchestra, the girls' friends the Music Fairies, was filling the air with lilting music.

"Now we shall introduce you to
the Princess Fairies properly," said
Queen Titania to Rachel and Kirsty
as all the fairies gathered round.
"They're wearing beautiful
ballgowns for this special
occasion, and not their
regular fairy outfits!"

Bertram led the
first Princess Fairy
into the ballroom.

"Welcome,
Princess Honor the
Happy Days Fairy!"
the queen announced.

Rachel and Kirsty
and all the other fairies
curtseyed as Princess Honor
waved and smiled. She wore a white

silk ballgown with crystal embroidery,
and a sparkling tiara set with a diamond
on her dark hair. The queen then
introduced Princess Demi
the Dressing-Up
Fairy, Princess
Anya the Cuddly
Creatures Fairy,
Princess Elisa
the Adventure
Fairy, Princess
Lizzie the
Sweet Treats
Fairy, Princess
Maddie the
Playtime Fairy and
Princess Eva the Enchanted
Ball Fairy.
Everyone broke into loud applause.

But all of a sudden a freezing blast of icy wind swept through the ballroom, making everyone shiver. The music crashed to a halt and all the candles blew out.

"Beware, everyone!" shouted King Oberon, holding onto his crown as the frozen wind swirled around them and icicles formed on the chandeliers. "This is one of Jack Frost's magical ice-bolts!"

Rachel and Kirsty glanced at each other in dismay. They were even more horrified when they noticed that all the Princess Fairies' beautiful ballgowns had turned to tattered rags. At that moment the ballroom doors were flung open. In strolled Jack Frost and a pair of goblins wearing their footman disguises.

"Surprise!" sneered Jack Frost, throwing his cap to the floor.

Tiara Thieves!

Rachel, Kirsty and everyone in the ballroom ducked as Jack Frost raised his wand and sent another ice bolt spinning towards them. The Princess Fairies cried out in shock as their glittering tiaras were whipped away from their heads. In an instant the tiaras flew through the air and landed on the heads of the goblins.

Jack Frost roared with laughter while the goblins looked very smug and began preening themselves.

"Who's a princess now?" cackled one goblin.

"WE ARE!" chorused the others proudly.

"Please give our tiaras back," Princess Honor pleaded.

"Our tiara magic isn't just for the things we look after," Princess Anya explained. "We Princess Fairies are responsible for *all* fairy magic. Without our tiaras, no human or fairy will ever have a happy or magical time again!"

"Good," Jack Frost retorted. "I want everyone to be miserable! We're going to hide away in the human world, and you Princess Fairies will never see your magic tiaras again – ha ha ha!" And lifting his wand, he fired a third ice bolt straight at the goblins.

But Rachel and Kirsty saw Queen Titania point her own wand at the goblins, too. A magical bolt of pink and purple mist shot towards them just as Jack Frost and the goblins disappeared with shouts of triumph.

"I didn't manage to stop them disappearing to the human world," Queen Titania explained, "But my magic has made sure that they will end up at Golden Palace!"

Rachel and Kirsty also noticed that the queen's magic had made the Princess Fairies' ragged ballgowns vanish. Each of them was now wearing a new outfit.

"Girls, we shall need your help once more to get the Princess Fairies' tiaras back," the queen went on. "All fairy magic depends on it!"

"We'll do our best," Kirsty promised, and Rachel nodded in agreement. All the fairies looked relieved.

"The Princess Fairies will help you in your search," King Oberon told them. "But first you girls should go back and get a good night's sleep."

"Goodnight, Rachel and Kirsty. We'll see you again soon!" the fairies called as another wave of the queen's wand sent the two girls whizzing off to Golden Palace.

Back in their chamber Rachel and Kirsty quickly unpacked and got ready for bed.

"Can you believe the cheek of Jack Frost, gatecrashing the fairies' ball?" Kirsty said sleepily as she snuggled under the covers.

"Well, we'll be ready for him tomorrow!" Rachel replied with a yawn.

However, when Rachel woke up next morning, she felt very out of sorts.

"I haven't had a good night's sleep at all!" she said grumpily to Kirsty. "This mattress is really lumpy. I wonder if there's something hidden underneath, like in *The Princess and the Pea*."

Kirsty sat up and
began scratching her
arms. "My quilt is
really itchy," she
grumbled. "I wish
it wasn't, because
I'm so fed up –
I feel like hiding
underneath it
all day!"

The girls still hadn't cheered up by the
time they'd washed, dressed and gone
down to breakfast.

Meals were served on long wooden
tables covered with white cloths in the
grand banqueting room which was hung
with beautiful tapestries. But this morning
no one looked as if they were enjoying
themselves very much at all.

"I don't *want* a royal breakfast of crumpets and bacon," one boy said sulkily. "I just want my favourite cereal!"

"My orange juice isn't orangey enough!" another girl complained. "And these crumpets have too much butter."

"Oh, Kirsty, I've just realised what's happening!" Rachel murmured in her friend's ear. "Everyone's miserable because Honor the Happy Days Fairy has lost her tiara."

Kirsty nodded. "Let's hope we find it soon," she replied, "Otherwise everyone's holiday at Golden Palace is going to be ruined!"

After breakfast Louis and Caroline
took them all into the library. It was a
magnificent room with huge mahogany
bookcases filled with leather-bound
books, but everyone still looked very glum.

"Right, we thought we'd act out some
prince and princess stories," Caroline said,
trying to sound cheerful. "We'll start with
Cinderella! That'll be fun, won't it?"

No one said anything.

"And we even have some pretend glass
slippers, too !" Louis whisked a pair of

high-heeled
shoes out of
a nearby
cupboard
and held
them up on
a cushion.

Caroline gave the children different parts to play, even though none of them were very enthusiastic at all. Rachel and Kirsty were guests at the prince's ball, and they watched as the girl playing Cinderella ran off at the stroke of midnight, leaving her glass slipper behind. But when the boy playing the prince asked everyone to try on the glass slipper, it didn't fit anyone, not even Cinderella herself!

"I don't understand," complained Cinderella, trying to force her foot into the shoe. "It fitted me just a little while ago!"

"Everything's going wrong," the prince said sadly. "This isn't the right ending to the story."

"Yes, and we know why!" Kirsty whispered in Rachel's ear.

"OK, maybe we should try something else," Louis suggested, glancing a little anxiously at Caroline. "Why don't you get into pairs and write your *own* stories?"

"It's a lovely sunny day, so go and explore the gardens for inspiration," Caroline said as she and Louis handed out velvet-covered notebooks and gold pens. "We'll all meet up later to share our stories."

Rachel and Kirsty went out of the library and headed towards the gardens along with everyone else. But as they passed the grand staircase, Kirsty caught Rachel by the arm.

"Rachel, look at the portrait of Princess Charlotte," Kirsty said in a low voice. "There's a golden light shining from behind it!"

As everyone else went out, the girls hung back, gazing up at the bright light. Then a fairy fluttered out from behind the painting and danced through the air towards them.

"It's me, girls!" called Princess Honor the Happy Days Fairy, "I'm here to search for my magical tiara. Will you help me?"

"Of course we will!" Rachel and Kirsty cried.

Green Fingers!

"Thank you, girls," Honor said gratefully. She now wore a beautiful red chiffon shift dress with a large bow on the front, and delicate gold shoes. "Where do you think we should start looking?"

"We're supposed to be going into the gardens," Kirsty told her, "So maybe we should start there."

Honor nodded. She flew down and slipped out of sight under the collar of Rachel's jacket. Then the girls followed the others outside.

The gardens looked even more beautiful in the spring sunshine than when the girls had seen them from the coach the previous day. Daffodils and tulips nodded their heads in the warm breeze, and the marble fountains were sending sparkling sprays of water into the air. But still Rachel and Kirsty didn't feel like smiling. Neither did any of the other children who were wandering around the lush green lawns looking rather grumpy.

"See that peacock?" said Kirsty, pointing the bird out to Rachel. The peacock was walking down one of the gravel paths, its tail feathers firmly closed and drooping on the ground. "He looks exactly how I feel!"

"Oh dear," Honor murmured, sounding distressed. "Everyone should be having a wonderful time here at Golden Palace. We *must* find my tiara, girls!"

Keeping a sharp eye out for the missing tiara, Rachel and Kirsty went over to join some of the children. They were staring at the topiary figures that the gardeners had clipped out of the thick leafy hedges.

"Look, there's a prince and a princess," Rachel said, pointing at two green figures with crowns on their heads. The prince wore knickerbockers and the princess a crinoline. "And here's a teddy bear, too!"

"This one is a witch," Kirsty added, admiring a very complicated topiary of a figure in a pointed hat sitting on her broomstick. "Rachel, maybe these characters would be good for our story?"

Rachel nodded. "Let's see what others there are," she suggested. "Look, there are some gardeners working on new figures at the end of that hedge."

The group of gardeners was clipping away at the branches of the hedge, intent on the shape they were making. Rachel and Kirsty went to look, but along the way they peered under all the hedges to see if they could spot the tell-tale magical sparkle of Honor's missing tiara. But there was nothing.

The gardeners had on sun-hats with very large brims that covered their faces. Rachel also noticed that they had very big feet. She began to look at them suspiciously.

Then one of the gardeners pulled off his gardening glove, tilted back the brim of his hat and scratched his long green nose with his finger.

"These gardeners really *do* have green fingers!" Kirsty exclaimed, "Because they're goblins in disguise!"

"And look," Honor whispered, "They're clipping the hedge into a figure of Jack Frost holding his ice wand!"

As Honor and the girls watched, the goblins finished sculpting Jack Frost's head and stood back proudly to admire their work. Quickly, Rachel and Kirsty ducked behind the hedge opposite.

"I wonder if they have the tiara with them," Kirsty said in a low voice.

"Let's listen in to their conversation and find out!" Honor suggested. "It'll be easier to stay out of sight if I turn you into fairies, girls."

Rachel and Kirsty nodded. A few swishes of Honor's wand sent a stream of fairy sparkles whirling around them, and instantly the girls shrank right down until they were exactly the same size as Honor, with the same gauzy wings. Then the three friends fluttered out from

behind the hedge. Quietly Honor led them over to the topiary figure of Jack Frost. The goblins had moved on to a new part of the hedge, and were discussing what shape to clip next. Putting her finger to her lips, Honor landed silently on the branch that formed Jack Frost's icicle beard. Rachel and Kirsty joined her.

"Let's make this bit of the hedge into the shape of Jack Frost's Ice Castle," suggested one of the goblins with a grin.

A second goblin nodded. "This is much more fun than that silly maze we got lost in," he remarked.

"Yes, but it was a good idea to hide that magical tiara in the middle of the maze, wasn't it?" the first goblin replied. "Those pesky fairies will never find it there, ha ha!"

Into the Maze

Honor, Rachel and Kirsty glanced at each other in delight. The tiara was hidden in the maze!

"It was *my* idea to put it there," boasted the second goblin.

"No, it was *me* who thought of it, actually!" snapped a third goblin.

Leaving the goblins squabbling as they clipped away at the hedge, Honor, Rachel and Kirsty zoomed off towards the maze. It was close by the topiary garden.

"It will be easy to spot the middle of the maze from above," Honor said as they flew over the twisting and turning rows of thick hedges. "We won't get lost, girls!"

But as Honor and the girls neared the centre of the maze, they heard the sound of gruff voices.

"That sounds like more goblins!" Kirsty whispered, pulling a face.

"They must have been left behind to guard the tiara," said Rachel.

Quickly Honor and the girls swooped down towards the middle of the maze and hid themselves in a dense patch of leaves. They peered out and immediately spotted two goblins. One of them was posing with Honor's tiara sparkling on his head, while the other was intent on sculpting a topiary figure of him,

complete with tiara.
Rachel, Kirsty and
Honor tried not to
give themselves away
by laughing.

As the second goblin finished
off his topiary, the goblin wearing the
tiara rushed forward to take a closer look.
He was now standing very near to where
Rachel was concealed in the hedge.

"You've made my nose too big!" the
tiara-wearing goblin snapped sulkily.

"No, I haven't," the other retorted. "It *is*
big – it's huge!"

Rachel saw her chance. She flew out
of the hedge and, hovering in the air, she
reached down to lift the tiara from the
goblin's head. But to Rachel's dismay, the
other goblin spotted her.

"Pesky fairy!" he howled, glaring at Rachel. Then he turned to his friend. "Run for it!" he shouted.

As Honor and Kirsty flew out of the hedge to join Rachel, the goblins took to their heels. One went left and one went right.

"Fly after the one who has the tiara!" Honor told Rachel and Kirsty. But when the goblin saw that they were following him, he took the tiara off.

"Catch!" he roared and flung it over the hedge to the other goblin who was running along behind it.

Honor, Rachel and Kirsty flew over
to him, but instantly the goblin chucked
the tiara under the hedge, back to the
other one.

"This is impossible!" Rachel panted as
the goblins continued to race around the
maze, flinging the tiara from one to the
other as if it was a ball. "How on earth
are we going to get the tiara back?"

Kirsty made a grab for the tiara as one
of the goblins tossed it over a hedge, but
it sailed right past her. Chuckling smugly,
the other goblin caught it and scuttled off.

"Can't catch me!" he boasted, waving
the tiara around.

Kirsty glanced desperately around
for inspiration and her gaze fell on the
topiary goblin.

"Oh!" she exclaimed. "I have an idea!"

Happy Days are Here Again

Quickly Kirsty whispered her plan to Honor and Rachel who smiled and nodded.

"We'll have to distract the goblins, Rachel, while Honor works her magic!" Kirsty told her friend.

The girls flew after the goblins, drawing them away from the centre of the maze.

Kirsty glanced back over her shoulder and saw Honor point her wand at the topiary goblin. A magical mist of fairy

dust surrounded it, and immediately the goblin made of leaves and twigs turned into a *real* goblin!

"Everything's going to plan," Kirsty thought, delighted.

"Hey, you two!" called a gruff voice. Kirsty and Rachel exchanged a smile as the goblins spun round. The girls knew that Honor was using her magic to make her voice sound goblin-like! "Throw the tiara to me right away – or those pesky fairies will have it!"

"Here, take it!" shouted the goblin with the tiara, hurling it through the air.

The topiary goblin caught the tiara neatly, but as he did so, he began to turn back to leaves and twigs again. Kirsty and Rachel flew forward and caught the tiara before it fell to the ground. Then Honor fluttered out to join them. The two goblins groaned loudly as they realised that they'd been tricked.

"What's Jack Frost going to say?" one of them mumbled crossly as they stomped away.

"And how are we going to find our way out of this maze?" the other wanted to know.

Kirsty and Rachel passed the tiara to Honor. As soon as she touched it, the tiara shrank down to its fairy-size, and Honor placed it carefully on her head. Rachel and Kirsty smiled.

"My magic is working already," Honor laughed, "That's the first time I've seen you smile all day, girls! And now everyone else will be happy, too. Thank you for your help. And now I must rush back to Fairyland and tell my princess sisters the great news! I know they'll be hoping that you'll help them find their tiaras, too."

"We'll do our best," Rachel promised as Honor whizzed off to Fairyland in a shower of rainbow-coloured fairy magic.

"We'd better go back to the library with everyone else," said Kirsty as they saw the other children on their way back into Golden Palace. As the girls hurried to join them, they saw that everyone was now chatting happily, smiling and laughing and obviously enjoying themselves.

"What a difference!" Rachel whispered to Kirsty.

Caroline and Louis were waiting in the library for them, and everyone settled down to write their stories.

"Let's write something really magical," Kirsty suggested. "We could have the princess from the portrait on the grand staircase as our heroine."

"Good idea," Rachel agreed, beginning to write.

"Right, shall we share some of our stories now?" Louis suggested after some time had gone by. "Rachel and Kirsty, would you like to go first?"

The girls stood up and, taking it in turns, they read out their story. It was about a princess called Charlotte who was sad because she'd lost her smile. But with the help of a talking peacock and a topiary teddy bear, she found it hidden in the middle of the maze. Everyone listened in rapt silence, and when Rachel and Kirsty finished, there was a round of applause.

"What a wonderful, magical story," Caroline said. "Well done."

"There's something about Golden Palace that almost makes you believe in magic!" said one of the girls, and Rachel and Kirsty grinned at each other.

"So, has everyone had a happy first day at Golden Palace?" asked Louis.

Everyone shouted "YES!" and cheered.

"And we've got another exciting adventure with the Princess Fairies to look forward to tomorrow!" Kirsty murmured to Rachel.

Now it's time for Kirsty and Rachel to help...

Demi the Dressing-Up Fairy

Read on for a sneak peek...

Kirsty and Rachel walked along the stone corridor with a group of children, all chattering excitedly. It was the second day of their holiday at Golden Palace, a beautiful castle in the countryside, and they were having a wonderful time. Golden Palace itself was amazing – it had been built from gleaming white stone hundreds of years ago, and had high towers topped with golden turrets. The owners of the palace were running a special 'Kids' Week' during the spring half-term, which included lots of different fun activities. Kirsty and Rachel were staying all week, and loved the fact that they were sleeping in a bedroom with a four poster bed where real princes and princesses had once slept before them!

That wasn't the only brilliant thing about their holiday here, though. Yesterday the girls had found themselves on a brand new fairy adventure – this time, helping the Princess Fairies look for their magical tiaras. The Princess Fairies were cousins of the King and Queen of Fairyland, and had been their special guests at a Fairyland Palace ball. But naughty Jack Frost and his mischievous goblins had invited themselves to the ball too – and had stolen the seven Princess Fairies' magical tiaras. The tiaras were full of powerful fairy magic, and without them, no human or fairy could have a happy or magical time.

"Come and see the palace's Jewel Chamber, guys," said Louis, one of the palace stewards who was looking after the children. "Through here."

Kirsty and Rachel followed the group into a small wood-panelled room, which had glass display cases arranged on the walls. "Wow," breathed Kirsty, as she peered in at the first case. "Lady Charlotte's christening bracelet from when she was a baby – a gift from the Spanish royal family, over two hundred years ago!"...

Read Demi the Dressing-Up Fairy to find out what adventures are in store for Kirsty and Rachel!

Meet the
Princess Fairies

Jack Frost has stolen the Princess Fairies' special tiaras.
Kirsty and Rachel must get them back, or all the magic
in the world will fade away!

Meet the fairies, play games
and get sneak peeks at
the latest books!

www.rainbowmagicbooks.co.uk

There's fairy fun for everyone at
www.rainbowmagicbooks.co.uk.
You'll find great activities, competitions, stories and
fairy profiles, and also a special newsletter.

Competition

you study this picture of the **Pet Keeper** Fairies you'll see that one
the seven friends is missing! Can you work out who it is? Make a
e of the first letter of the name of the missing fairy. When you have
oyed all seven books in the Princess Fairies series, arrange the seven
letters to make a special word, then send the answer in to us!

e will put all of the correct entries into a draw and select one
ner to receive a special Rainbow Magic Princess Fairies Pack!

Enter online now at

www.rainbowmagicbooks.co.uk

Natalie the Christmas Stocking Fairy

Jack Frost has taken the three magical items belonging to Natalie the Christmas Stocking Fairy. Kirsty and Rachel must get them back, or this year nobody will have any presents!

Out Nov 2012

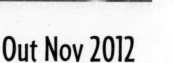